Footsteps

in Time

Journey to the far side of the dash ...

Poems
by

Beecher B Brown, Jr

I think Sonny can be designated the "People's Poet." His work exhibits a depth of sensitivity to and understanding of the human condition. He is thoughtful. He is perceptive.

R J Cowley Jr - Author

Imprint: Independently published

Imagery by Anne Beecham

Book layout by David P Schulze

All imagery used on the cover or within the following pages may be either original photos by the author or drawings, photos, composites from royalty-free stock image collections.

DEDICATION

To my wife Jeannie

Our children: Burt, Genifer, Ward, and Delta
Our grand and great grand children

My Mother Katherine Rigsby Brown
Father Beecher B Brown Sr (II)
My brothers Tom, Danny, Ron, John
My sisters Linda, Debbie
In memoriam: Ted, Barbara, Nancy, Terry, Larry

My neighbors Ken and Connie
My friend and mentor David Schulze
Rich Crowley for his encouragement,
Support and transport to and from
Writers Guild meetings

With special appreciation to
the Plantation Writers Guild
for their comments and critique

TABLE OF CONTENTS

POEMATIC EXPRESSION
David P Schulze

Poetry and stories are two different projections. Stories are delivered from the author's pen to the mind of the reader using strict syntactical constructions and punctuation guidelines for a richer, fuller experience in the delivery.

Poematic expression grants the artist "poetic license" to build meaning into verse and non-traditional structure that allows the reader to experience the presentation one word at a time.

Poetry is Expression
Communication
Read slowly

Savor the words
Absorb them
Feel them

Breathe
Live the moment
As the poet does

- *FORWARD* -

An excerpt from The DASH

(describing the mark between dates of
birth and death on a tombstone)

by Linda Ellis

*For that dash represents all the time they spent alive
on earth and now only now only those who loved them know
what that little line is worth.*

*For it matters not how much we own, the cars... the
house... the cash. What matters is how we live and love
and how we spend our dash.*

*So think about this long and hard; are there things
you'd like to change? For you never know how much
time is left that can still be rearranged.*

*To be less quick to anger
and show appreciation more
and to love the people in our lives
like we've never loved before.*

*If we treat each other with respect and more often
wear a smile... remembering that this special dash
might only last a little while.*

- *PROLOGUE* -

Perspective has been relative to me as its attributes affect those I love, care for and befriend in my journey through life. I never thought about historical effects to be inherited or bequeathed or of its significance in the generational recycling of life that helps us as human being to be more like our Creator than any other creature or species.

Each generation begins anew with a link to a chain of love, lust or happenstance that gives us our own peculiar DNA and circumstance to begin and develop our individual stories to connect our link to the next generation. The dash on our tombstone separating birth and death will only be dissimilar than that on all the other tombstones throughout eternity by the story we leave behind symbolized by that dash. Like a gain of sand on a beach our dash appears to be meaningless, insignificant, until it is realized all the beaches of the world are built one grain at a time.

I was researching my namesake grandson's ancestors. Me, my wife and my son, his wife and all brothers, sisters, relatives, etc, precede him in this chain of love. As I checked through the dashes of the fathers of each generation of his great, great grandmother's ancestors I ultimately went back twelve generations to Moses McCarter, born 1731 Roxbourhgshire, Scotland, died 1 February 1781, Abbeyville, South Carolina and I suddenly realized I had looked through a pile of dashes large enough to fill a space in time similar to the building of beaches on earth one grain at a time. And I had only looked at one ancestorial chain. The numbers are staggering.

What is the significance of this 290 years old bit of history today?

For me on the down hillside of my dash, close to forging the final bonding of my link in this chain of love I am reviewing, the value of legacy or lack thereof, in the life I have lived and what someone might see or learn to help them when making a similar review 290 years after they were born. It certainly makes the times in my life when I wondered about the worth of individuals and how we contribute come alive and point out the value in living a positive, joyful, caring and shared perspective regardless of hardships, depressions, recessions or maladies to be survived.

Conception is the beginning for a new link to be added in this multifaced spiderlike creation in chains of love expanding in the continuance of eternity. We should all want our link to hold a story far beyond the symbol of a dash on our tombstones.

LINKS OF LOVE

Time existed before birth
And will after death.
Our love cannot be
Confined to just our life times.
We are heirs
In a chain
Forged from passion
Lust
Building and rebuilding
Long
Before we were born.
We are
But connections
To be bequeathed
To the unborn.
Whenever and however
Love grows
It will exist
Beyond our
Momentary twinkle
In the void of time.

LIVING

What is it all about?

The dash on tombstones
appears insignificant until symbolized.
I have come to honor it as a lesson from my creator
Who provides mankind with imagination,
curiosity, intellect, and talents for expression
plus
the unknown, unseeable, untouchable elements of
FAITH, HOPE; LOVE
And consequence,
It represents value and worth
Or opposites
in life
Second only to the dash being seen
When a line is drawn through its middle
To form a cross.

Generations from now
my descendants can view my dash
and know without the story between
date of birth and death
neither their ancestors
or possible lineage of descendants
would exist
if it were not
for me.

How many will that simple truth impact
Because of
my dash?
Stack all the stories of ancestors
And of descendants yet
to come
With their beginnings
The same as mine
And my individual
Miniscule story to be told
Is valuable
Important
Worthy of celebration
And inspiration
As is each story
Awaiting discovery.

Birth and Death
Are cold hard facts.
If nothing else conception
is existence in the space of time
and that is the shortest story
between the dash.

Worthy, glorious
Detrimental, unworthy …

No matter

Wonderful.
Horrible
Normal
Impactful
Unlimited stories abide
Like stars shining, twinkling
Hiding mysteries in the
Cyclical return of nights.

How bright or dim
Will our stories shine
in the revolution
of the universe.
That story will be told
on the downhill side of the dash
where existence
is revealed
Like stars hanging
In the sky
Bright
Dim
Or not at all ...
Lost or Found
in the impartiality
Of time.

Footsteps in Time

Journey to the far side of the dash ...

Poems
by

Beecher B Brown, Jr

- TIME PASSES -

PICTURES PAINTED
BY THE HANDS OF TIME

The cyclical nature of seasons
began when I was born.
Like lilies in water
Blooms on flowers
I flowered for all to see
And fawn over me.
Resurrection
Salvation on the cross
Promises of eternal life
Is what Spring signifies
For me,

Summers are fun
Running and playing
daydreaming in the sun
Watching grain growing
seeds planted
Watered and fertilized.
Sweating and swimming and growing.
Nights, stars, the milky way
Were made for me
to visualize otherwise
unseeable unthinkable things
in the depository of my mind

Fall a time
for harvesting Pumpkins
tricks or Treat
World Series and football
Thanksgiving,
Turkey Dressing
cranberry sauce
Family praying
celebrating around the table.
Preparation
For winter's call
And challenges.

Winter a time for sheltering
And enjoying comfort of
Blankets
a furnace
Christmas and the birth of Jesus
Joy with family
Peace on Earth
Good will to men
Merry Christmas
Happy New Year.

Yellows, browns,
whites and reds
purple, greens of the days
Cycles come. Cycles go.
I used to think Spring
Foretold it all
Until I discovered
The hint of death
Melancholy of nostalgia
In the colors of the Fall.

The Master
Paints this countryside
In a gallery for display
But He has given it
Dimmed eyes, grey beard
Bifocals and bunions
And a tick in the toc of time
Which will soon
Be passed on
In a cycle never ending
As long as
Newer generations
Are born.

The Master blesses me
With his brush.
I have become a portrait
For display,
I no longer associate
With butterfly collections
Or flowers in a vase.
I am but a link in
A chain of love
To be displayed with all the links
scattered
In eternity's infinity.

EVOLUTION

ADOLESCENCE

          Greener grass

MIDDLE AGE

          Pastures

OLD AGE

          Barn full of hay

THE CORNER

Love, laughter ...
Tears, despair ...
Life - death ...
All of human emotion
awaits us
just around the corner.
The influence of each
and what they have to teach
only varies
with the time we linger
before we decide
to turn the corner.

CHAIN OF LOVE

If time exists
before and after death,
my love cannot
be confined
to just my lifetime.
Love is not
a mere one time
happening.
It may be born
in dreams,
but it survives
midst the cloudy
atmosphere
of life's realities.
So I am an heir
in a chain of love
hate, lethargy
and incentive
formed long before
I was born,
and I am but
a connecting link
to be bequeathed
to those yet unborn.

Time cannot be seen
but it is felt,
and I know
wherever or whenever
I go
my love will exist
in infinity
and not just be
a momentary twinkle
in a void of time
or a mere progression
in futility.

DISCOVERY

Unto each a season,
What would Capistrano be
Without the swallows

The center line divides a journey by half
And dead ends are only reached
When we refuse to turn around.
Detours ..,
Ah, detours
What would shadows in the mind conceal
Without those junctures
Plateaus
Where decisions are made
Superhighways
Through which
Fertile fields of wonder
Are discovered
On the other side of
Congested stop signs
Right of ways yielded
And beyond the light of caution
Reflecting memories from the color red
When green was the only way to go.

Consequences
Oh, consequences
Life lasting, threatening

Controlling
What might have been
Could have …
What is.

How? How?   How?

Dreams should not be forsaken
For questions that never end.
Hope is more than the unknown
Hiding behind the illusions
Of life's dead ends

It rains. I dream of Sunny skies.
I cry. I recall, seek, need laughter.
Depression settles in
But I have known the uphill side
Of such conditioning
Pain is a bitter, jealous, selfish
Psychosis
Or a conditioning
Forging, growing
Metamorphosis
Leading to dreams
Substance to life
And direction to
Fields of wonder yet be wandered.

I WANDER

Sitting wondering
why no specifics
will come out
I find myself lost
in pressure, a headache,
too many cigarettes smoked
and too much coffee drunk.
The times of wandering
midst amazement,
serendipity
and astonishment
where wandering was
a journey of the senses
being alive
and joy abounded
undisguised
where words came easily
because there was
neither will nor want
to think
are, at least,
temporarily gone.

I feel ... feel ...
what do I feel?

A need, burning desire,
to express anxiety
frustration, fears ...?

Am I delving in
boredom?
Questioning?
Is my faith
being tested?

Fear? Yes.
I feel fear.
Worry? Yes.
I am worried.

Whatever is
badly, broken, bent
and in arrears
is far ahead
of where I am at.
Murphy's Law
only begins to describe
the story of my life,
and effects of
consequence on those
who love and are loved
by me.

My heart is breaking.
Not for what
might have been
but for what is
and because tomorrow
promises no more
than more of the same.
Am I crazy?
Why don't I
give up
and stop thinking?
Why are the thoughts
so damned difficult
to organize?
Why
when every logical
process in
my mind's circuitry
says to dig ditches,
wash windows
or shovel cow manure
do I expend
so much energy thinking?

I have to do it.
I am an addict.
It is inherent -
not compulsive.
It is breathing,
sleeping, dreaming.

I am lost ...
No better than when
I began.
Headache.
Heartburn.
I think,
I attempt
to express,
but aimlessly
I wander.

BLOOD PRESSURE

Blood pressure, anxiety, tension
frustration, depression, regression
are symptoms
conditioning
more of the same.
Change is feared
because the unknown
overwhelms wanting better
A stagnate comfortableness is found
though the journey
is predestined to go wrong.

If subject to such conditioning
laughter, joy
warmth, tenderness
sharing, happiness
would come along
more often.
Miracles comes true
We fail or see them
midst glaring lights
blaring noise
Ignoring
extraordinary
occurring
in the mundane boredom
of the ordinary

TWILIGHT ZONE

We look back.
We look ahead.
But, now
is all the time
there is.
Both memories
and dreams
exist in now,
and if
we try to get
too far ahead
or end up
too far behind
we misuse
the only time
there is -

- *TIME STANDS STILL* -

TODAY IS

Know what today is
  ?

The 1st day of
  the rest
    of our
      lives ...

Time when
  the potential
    for a miracle
      exists ...

Space
  for sharing
    caring
      giving ...

Opportunity
  for experiencing
    and extending
      forbearance
        patience
          forgiveness ...

An easel
   for painting
      a work of art
       founded
         in faith ...

A score
   for
     composition
      of a song
       to be sung
        for our
          lifetimes ...

A piece of granite
   to be chiseled
    into a statue
     preserving
      the concept
       of hope ...

A page
   in a book
    for recording
     the wisdom
      of learning

A field
  of wonder
    to be
      wandered ...

A scale
  of descending
    moments
      of joy
        to be
          experienced
          and
            explored ...

An arena
  for challenge
    to be
      overcome ...

A forum
  for
    the discovery
      of
        serendipity ...

A source
    of magical
    power
        to ignite
            the ordinary
                with
                    the electricity
                        of
                            spontaneity ...
Today is
    a celebration
    of living
        and loving
            you.

TOMORROW IS CANCELLED

Tomorrow is cancelled
As yesterdays accumulate
But today
Oh, today
Is the most interesting.
The past is for
Definition
And proceeding from
The future for
Dreaming
And proceeding to
But all that
Transpires
Is in the theater
Of today.
We enter
And exit
On a day.
So, live as if
Today Is all there is
Will ever be
From time
Beginning
To ending
Today is
All there is.

OH!

The joy
The indescribable joy
Of trusting and loving
Without reservation
Without worry
Or hiding from doubts
Of just being as we are
sometimes together
Sometimes apart
Secure in knowing
The gentle breeze of
Compassion
Will interpret
And
Soothing antidotes
Of forgiveness
Will bathe
our weaker moments
With understanding.

- WHAT IS IN A DAY -

TO BE EXCHANGED

What is in a day?

Some say nothing,
others opportunity,
some
have no opinion
at all,
and it may be
each is right.

After three cardiac arrests
And eighty-one years
I say each to his own.

A day contains
no more or less
than what
we are willing
to exchange it for.
And,
exchanged
it must be.

POTENTIAL

What is in a day?

I investigate
Measure
And attempt to categorize potential
For love and hate
Productivity and waste.
In summary
I am surprised.
Recapitalization shows
It is not who I think I am
But who I have become
And who I am to become
Who is important.

OPPORTUNITY

What is in a day?

Opportunity … love
Being born, dying…growing
Based in hope
Pain, guilt
Or as in times like now
Certainty.

FULFILLMENT

What is in a day?

Excitement, challenge,
fulfillment - love -
both given and received,
and sometimes
taken away.
At one point a day
is brief,
at another eternity
and, yet, at another
time ignored.

BOREDOM, SORROW, DOUBT

What is in a day?

Boredom, sorrow, doubt,
discontent - love
wanted, unwanted
and misplaced.

On a given day
it is great,
on another, despair
and, yet, on another
each combined.

CHOICES

We are conceived,
born and die,
in a day.
All that transpires
in between
is a day to day
trade off ...
a day to day
progression
in discernment,
communication
and choice.
Thus,
the choices
are important to me

MISTAKES

Mistakes
have to be made
proceeded from,
and I choose
to cast the die
consciously.
I want to face
our tomorrows
without regret
because
I must
live with and accept
our consequence.

DEPARTURE

Conception, birth, death
Occurs on its day.
All transpiring between each
Is day to day trade off.
God designed us to perceive
Make choices
And to communicate.
As I flirt with departure
Every day is important.
After the fact
Tomorrow's regrets
Will be for someone else to tell
And will end my soliloquy.

CONVALESCENCE

Conception, birth and death are each unto its day.

All in between is a day to day trade off

Because each day contains no more
Than we are willing to exchange it for
And exchanged it must be.

In His image
God designed us to perceive
make choices and communicate.
Let's progress toward the what and when
Of the unknown
Sharing wine food and laughter
Tinged with fears, tears and sadness of tragedy.
Perhaps together we can find a bit of happiness.
Let's make each day important
Face tomorrow without regret
And maybe this time
Will be tempered by
The kindness we share.

What is in a day ...

but struggle, work
Opportunity
For us to love
Beyond compare.

- *PERCEPTION* -

GLASS HOUSES

A sugar bowl is only full
of sweetness
so long as it is filled
with sugar.
Fill it with salt
suddenly
it develops
the deceptiveness of people
who must be sampled frequently
before we have any idea
of who or what
they really are.
To presuppose
what love should be
is to build a fishbowl
around our lives,
and even the largest aquariums
are awfully small
once we have seen, smelled, or dreamt
of the sea.

L-O-V-E

L – is for listening to what I meant
Not what I said.

O – is for being only you
Without pretense.

V – is for understanding the vulnerability
Between love that grows
And that which stagnates.

E – is for every time we meet
And though it's last
It is never least.
It stands for things like
The e's in
Forever …
Endless…
Eternity…

FUEL FROM MEMORIES

Light may be
At the end
of the tunnel
And silver may be
An outlined reflection
From some distant far off
Sun shrouded cloud
But hope is never any further away
than fringes of despair.
Hope is born and grows
Midst tears and fears
Depression
And is never any further away
Than perception
In a kaleidoscopic potpourri
Of anxiety and worry.
It is a catalyst far greater than
The whimsy of dreams.
Hope derives fuel from memories
Is purpose from wanting to be
Reason for being
That chisels appreciation
From the impossibility of now
For what is yet to be.

A BLANK AND STARING CANVAS

- a memory-
not from lack of anything
to be painted
but from uncertainty...
uncertainty about value,
perception and interpretation...
not interpretation from intent
but rather how
how will my transmission
be received.

I paint.
Oh, how I paint.
The materials are free.
It is in consequence
where the price is paid.

I am a manipulator -
a user of tools-
but not even I know
what the results will be.
Frequently
the mildest pastels
have the most violent degree
and the broad, bold and colorful
strokes so powerfully conceived
have so little impact
that not even I can believe.

Laughter identifies with
happiness.
I love to laugh
but at the wrong times
and at the wrong things
the images portrayed
are pain, tears
and rationalization -
apologies and explanations-
entirely different than
those for which ...
I laughed.

Patience, forgiveness -
tolerance -
are assets to be admired,
but it is a terrible shock
and tormenting to the ego
to find their expression
interpreted as liabilities
subject to criticism
and weaknesses inadequate
to dispel clouds
of depression.

Wanting, needing -
producing-
are characteristics
said to be necessities
in our society.

But, when after the labor
and sacrifice of trying
results in constant
emotional crises,
the twisted, distorted
and painful reflections
of good intent so gone awry
interfere with the attempts
to display images
that are good.

Faith, trust - confidence
I fall back on.
From having been
so misunderstood
I begin to perceive
the conception
of understanding.
I fight cynicism, doubt - fear.
It is so easy
for them to seep in.
I must be aware
of what I cultivate.

Weeds grow easily.
It is natural to assume
they are more
than what they are.
Dried flower arrangements
are beautiful and more tempting

to paint than a field of corn.
But I must not dwell only
in that which is
pleasing to my senses
or that which immediately
appears all consuming to
my emotions.

What I want to paint
lies within my attitude.
It must reflect dreams
as well as memories,
hope as well as insecurities
and it must be a sharing
rather than a hiding -
a sharing of emotional maturity
rather than a seeking
of solutions for anyone other
than myself.

Where the painting occurs
is not subject to a telling
or demand in anyone else's
acceptance or rejection.
These are definitions
which occur
in peace and security
or fear and instability
inside me individually.

My only responsibility
is the care and concern
with which I paint
and for the emotions
stirred inside me
where the paintings
are conceived for expression.

I shall paint in conception
never known before
and hopefully the bits
and pieces of me
will better fit the imaginations
on which I paint
better than before.
The materials are free.
Hopefully the consequence
will improve so the results
are pleasing for all who dare
to share with me.

OBSESSION

I am like a nuclear reactor
with all its cooling rods withdrawn.
My meltdown is long overdue.
Three Mile Island
is about to reoccur.

I am like Mt. St Helens.
I am about to explode
from my dormant stagnated
crater of suppressed spontaneity
into a moment of serendipity.

But when?

I think.
I dream.
I feel.
Yet, I do not know
what to say
or what the aftermath
will be.

Depending on how I view it
my life is either
a soap opera or
a magnificent obsession.

The masters have expressed
nothing that I
to some greater or lesser
degree
have not experienced.
Does it matter
unless it is expressed?

I am filled with hope ...
yet awestruck
by the effort to confine
my wandering kaleidoscopic
thoughts
to a specific which
regardless of consequence
can come out.

Results may be shared,
appreciated, loved,
grown from, hated, abused
or regressed from
but the true measurement
of genius
is imparting perception
into expression,
and a painting, sculpture
symphony or poem
is only a partial expression
of the greatness
motivating both perception
and creation into
tangible reality.

In feelings, imagination,
love and paradoxes
I know the devils,
demons, dreams and
aspirations
of my disposition
are uniquely me.
In spite of my
outward acquiescence to life,
inside I view
the ordinary extraordinarily
and somehow
I am going to express
the pent-up boiling
forces erupting
inside of me.

STRANDED

Lies, threats, cheating,
tears, fears, disappointments ...
a broken heart ...
Being stranded in a sea
of loneliness, guilt, revenge,
jealousy, selfishness
are all easier to overcome
than one illusion of truth
killing hope and saying
change cannot be for the better.

FLASHBACK PARADOXES

I remember many years ago
an effort to bring out of my consciousness
an idea, my thoughts ...
an expression as it appeared in
my imagination,
but it was lost in the blackness
of infinity
as my perception and vocabulary
struggled with the emptiness
of inexperience.
Now, right now, I face a similar
dilemma but
in reverse.
Infinity now appears so crowded
with past ups and downs,
current joys and sorrows
and future hopes and doubts
that to choose from the variety
is being lost in a kaleidoscope
of diversity
overshadowing specifics
with a maze of stimuli
so entwined that it appears
impossible
for any specific to be extracted
from the whole.

Sunshine, fog
rain - desert heat,
anger
love, hate - peace,
tears, smiles, laughter
anguish
paradoxes
I exist and subsist
on flashback paradoxes.
So, when expression does come out
with any concise clarity
I am conditioned and motivated
to investigate the influence
of its yet to be expressed
counterpart.
I know not the luxury
of 100% right
or 100% wrong.
I am without excuse
of 75% commitment
or 75% prejudice.
I am not blinded by fear
or bound by vision.
At times, I am
more observer than participant,
but always I am
a recorder,
but not like a computer.
I feel. I am alive.

My lack of logic
as well as my ability to perceive
is as much of my
uniqueness
as is my desire
to be unique.
So, inspite of all the experience,
I return to where I began ...
the emptiness ...
the lack of perception,
vocabulary ...
the inability to express
the beauty and the worth
of what is most unique -
the extraordinary
ordinary.

ODE TO AN OLD FART

Since way back when
everything
Was perfect ... ly
Not what it seemed,
I've been up a lot of downs
And out a lot of ins
To only arrive at where
I never anticipated being
From where
I never expected to leave

To have entered and exited
Only as directed
Or to have survived
Only for the expected
Would have spoiled
the aging of this wine.
I came from dust
To leave footprints
In the wilderness
of time
So
As I return
from whence I came
Let it be known
I am a dusty
Never
A dirty old man.

PROMISE, MYSTERY, DESIRE

Promise, mystery, desire
Chisel to stone
Paint to canvass
Notes to music
Pen to paper
Can never tell me
What you describe with your eyes.
Concisely, clearly ... directly
They speak.
You speak through a medium
overshadowing
the conversation
we are having.
The invitation
makes worry go away
disappointments disappear
and magic feelings come alive.
Feelings!
My God Feelings.
I revel in the touch of your eyes.
as they bind me with a spell ...
promise, mystery, desire.

- SAGE OF LIFE -

SOMEWHERE - SOMETIME

Are there still
pictures to paint?

Rainbows to chase?

Fields of wonder
to wander?

Is imagination
so dulled,
hope so resigned
and beauty so cloaked
by the familiar
that previously
unseen, unheard ...
unstirred feelings
cannot be grown?

Is it possible
these fields
become unfertile
because seeds
for germination
are ignored
for fields of fear
doubt, cynicism
and resignation
within
perceptions status quo?

Where to go?
How to go?

May not be
immediately answerable,
but looking back
and looking ahead
we always end up
somewhere - somehow,
and if
God allows us breath
and thought on earth,
expressions of joy
and genius
are only non-existent
as we so allow
their incarceration
within ourselves
individually.

DESTINY IS BIRTH

Dying
And all between
Is a part
Called fate

Control
Is kept
Or frittered away
In consequence
And responsibilities
Within
Prescribed boundaries
Of status quo fate.

HANDICAPS

Handicaps are not
Always physical and mental.
A cripple isn't
Just one who cannot walk.
Eyes for seeing
Ears for listening
Mind for assimilating
(Translating
Communicating)
Tongue for talking
But none before
The first three are used.

ECCENTRICITY

The eccentricity
Of my nature
Is to achieve
Wealth and wisdom
To afford
Eccentricity

WISDOM

God grant me the serenity
to accept what I have bought
in the battles I have fought;
the courage to accept
the mistakes I thought
the battles had surpassed;
and the wisdom to distinguish
the point where questions
are no more than excuses in disguise
for lies I once thought
honestly to be truth.

SEEKING HUMILITY

I have made every mistake
I was capable of.
Yet,
though much of life
appears to be crumbling,
I am not bitter,
I am not cynical,
and I am searching
for a new way - a how -
to proceed.

I love deeper, stronger
than ever before,
my faith is confirmed.
I bless and seek God's guidance
rather than blame or deny
His existence for my failures.

Care, concern and hope
for family
now have meaning
I never dreamed possible.
Though they suffer
from my mistakes

I pray for their understanding,
and for each of them
to develop a wisdom
and maturity to accept
the restrictions I impose
on their lives
by my limitations
as temporary.

I shall make more mistakes.
As I review the past
and preview the future
I have no resentment for either.
Choices were and shall
continue to be based
on information available
and maturity
at time of decision.
To wish differently
is useless.
Proceeding from the past
and to the future
is the only way to go.

THERE IN ...

I wish I knew the answers
to all your questions,
the solutions to all your problems,
but then
of what value
would there be in choice?

I do not, cannot,
and shall never possess
the wisdom or maturity
to be so omnipotent.
But maybe
therein lies
the basis
for both
wisdom and maturity.

God did not make us
each one way.
He gave us choice -
potential to create
or to destroy.
How we make and face
the consequence
is the uniqueness of
you and me.

Let's allow the right and room
for differences
as long as the differences
are not designed
to cripple one another.
Let's not push
pull and argue
the basic interrogatives
to convert the other
against his choice.
Let's merge our similarities,
grow because of our differences,
compromise on
our individual set
of consequences
and allow the other
their choice
their response
their request
their convictions
their confessions.
Therein lies
what we cherish
as unique.

FORESIGHT

If hindsight is better than foresight
Why does it delve so much in
What might have been
Rather than spurring us
To look ahead in fore thought.

LISTEN

Silence is golden ...
in its realm,
we found
true expression.

Silence is golden ...
in its reality,
we found language
mutually interpretable.

Silence is golden ...
through its wisdom,
we found sharing
not to be found in words.

Silence is golden ...
through the gentleness
of its voice,
love was heard
and understood.

- *FAMILY LIFE* -

REMEMBERING MOM

Katherine Virginia Rigsby Brown
April 15, 1921 – November 24. 1995

I could talk about my mother and the halo she now wears in heaven. I know what she would say to that.

"eech/shrug"

I could talk about her in terms of hard times she went through. I know what she would say about that.

"… eech/shrug"

I have had a hard time figuring out what to say that could be appropriate for both earthly goodbyes and our feelings of loss, grief and pain. Yet, I can hear her saying to me, "I love you." And that is what I am going to talk about. Her love for me and each of you … her children, in-laws, grandchildren, great grandchildren, relatives, and friends.

Every now and then God makes a special person who, regardless of birth, education or aspirations, is destined to be what HE intended them to be,

Moses, regardless of circumstance was destined to lead the chosen people into the promised land, to be a major author/figure of The Old Testament.

Paul was educated and chose to persecute the Christian people, but he was destined for conversion and is a major author in the books of the New Testament.

Our mother was not an extremely religious woman, But she was the most spiritual woman I have ever known; was destined to be a mother blessed with inner strength stronger than any metal known to science; and faith that survived more adverse circumstances that even I who went through those adverse circumstance with her can ever imagine, Never will I ever be able to imagine what it was like to wake up on a New Years day with ten children at home, pregnant with number 12, having absolutely no money, no food, fuel to heat the house. She not only survived ... she never complained ... and ten of those wonderful, happy, and productive children are here today. She was blessed with twenty-six grandchildren and twenty-three great grandchildren to add to this chain of love.

Our mother was a very human woman. She could be cantankerous ... ask any of her doctors. She could be stubborn. I'll let each of those who knew her tell their stories about that.

Her greatest virtue was simplicity, In a world where we have a tendency to complicate by needing more money, more cars, more fun, more houses ... more of everything '" she day by day needed food, clothing, shelter with no frills. But there was always a positive attitude, faith, and hope that if God could clothe the animals and feed the birds there was no question that she and her children would survive, and grow into loving, caring, and productive beings,

I never heard her say she deserved more, and if there was anything called poverty, it was a condition for someone other than her,

I could tell stories, but I shall leave those for times more appropriate when you can share your stories with me. Just remember our mother loved you when you were near, when you were away and that love does not go away with our saying goodbye today.

Look at the chain of love gathered here. Multiply it by years to come. Each of us are a part of her love to grow, pass on, and as long as infinity is … is as long as her love will last.

I am, supposedly, an educated man. I can philosophize, theorize and talk to the point of boredom. But you could talk to my mother for minutes and leave wondering why you felt good … knowing you'd learned something valuable you had overlooked somewhere in your life.

I know of no greater tribute I could pay than to say:

Mom
You loved me yesterday
Today
And beyond forever
In your wonderful
Loving way,,,

Our mother was a builder of bridges to places we once thought we could never go. They are bridges that cannot be seen or touched, but they have meanings inside and between each of us. The proof of their existence is the strength of the bonds forged because they do exist.

I shall read a poem dedicated not to her memory but to her life and all the lives yet to be built,

Let's celebrate the bridges
Burned, built and yet to be built.
We could get nowhere without the bridges
As long as our separate journeys were
And as many detours we had to make
We would not be at this intersection
But for the bridges constructed
Torn down and rebuilt again,

Bridges allow us opportunity to determine
If we are wise enough
To take water that ran away yesterday
Evaporated and falls again today
Drink of it and grow
Before it passes beneath the bridge
On which we stand.

Bridges span both space and time
And though the structure on which we stand
Is little more than a fallen log
It is from such fragile
Trusts and confidences
We span our gulf of doubt and fear
With love and hope
And more ahead than all we lost
When what was so important disappeared
Beneath a bridge that collapsed so long ago.
Bridges allow us to go back in memory
To look ahead in dreams
And there are many more to be built.

Our mother would say

Come
Go forward with me.
A rosebud cut and watered in a vase
Brings pleasure
And gives beauty for awhile
But planted in the ground
It spans seasons and years
With rhyme
I want to write building bridges
With you.

I love you all

Dad   Mom

REMEMBERING DAD

What could I say. It is hard to find words when traditional words do not apply.

My older brother Ted was born Dec 31, 1937. He was not named after dad. At his birth, dad was gone. Somewhere in Texas, I have been told. Mom had been abandoned, and had gone to live with Grandma and grandpa Rigsby to give birth at their home by lantern, candlelight, and midwife in Turtle town, Tn, midst the Tellico mountains in Polk county TN.

Dad must have been home when I was born on September 9. 1939 in Knoxville, TN. I was named after him. I was the 3rd Beecher, but my Grandfather disappeared when my father was a boy and was declared dead after seven years. My father assumed Sr. and I am listed as Jr. on my birth certificate.

In 1963 my son Beecher was born, and his birth certificate reads Beecher IV and his son Beecher V was born in 1992. After 1939, my mom had four daughters and six more sons, the last six in eight years. It is believed she had three or four miscarriages. The last child, John, was born June 6, 1959. Dad was gone for six months prior to his birth and was not heard from until 12 months later. This time he abandoned her pregnant with 9 children at home, no food, fuel for the wood and coal stoves, money, transportation, or telephone to live in a tiny tin roofed, 5 room house in the middle of a 40- 60 acre cow pasture.

With the birth of each child circumstance and consequence worsened and survival was the goal for existence. All twelve survived until our brother Larry was killed in a hit and run auto accident in 1978 in Baltimore, Md.

In addition to the abandonments, dad was an alcoholic and lived away from the family most of the time. When he was around, he was drunk, aggressive and abusive to the children. We grew up hating and dealing with fear. He did not whip us, he beat us. He worked mostly nights driving cabs or a wrecker truck. He would make us lay under his bed and stare at the dust on the bed springs, and beat the hell out of however many was crammed under the bed if anyone woke him up.

In later years, after moving the family to Baltimore, the oldest of the younger children physically threw him out of the house. A few of the oldest called the police and took him to court, none of which improved conditions unless he was gone.

Sometime in the early 1970s until 1980, he lived in and out of VA hospitals. He had a heart attack in his 40s and suffered with coronary artery, pulmonary and diabetes diseases until his death. In 1980, I picked him up at the VA hospital in Cincinnati. Ohio, and brought him to live at our house in Marietta, GA. After a year, the atmosphere became unbearable, and we moved him to public housing in Marietta.

At mine and one of my brother's encouragement, after a year, or so, my mother moved in with him to have a decent

and stable place to live. After a few years, his controlling behavior worsened until she left him, for the first time in their marriage, to live with our sister Nancy until she died, November 1995, in Culpepper. Virginia.

Dad then moved in with my sister Linda and her children for a couple of years. His diabetes worsened. He had both legs amputated. He was confined to a wheelchair. His mental and physical health continued to decline until his death in an old-soldiers home in Alabama.

Nine of his children, their spouses, a grandchild, my mentor and the minister from my childhood church, Cedar Bluff Baptist, were gathered, mostly at my request, to share our common conundrums about our feelings and the meaning and effects of our father on our lives.

"Dad"

Feb 1916 - April 6, 1995

Prayers are answered.

All of us. on one occasion or another, have prayed for God to help us ... and from Ted the oldest to John the youngest. there were times when we lived in Cedar Bluff, Tennessee and Baltimore, Maryland when we were in such circumstances that we could not foresee how we were going to survive, times when we asked God to deliver us.

Growing up in Cedar Bluff I went to Cedar Bluff Baptist church. Horace Hamilton was my Sunday School Teacher.

He has been my mentor throughout my life. He joins us to support us today, He requested the Revered Alan Simms from the church to conduct today's ceremony. He is our speaker today.

The church means more to me today. I am much more spiritual now, as compared to religious back then. Today I stand to witness prayers are answered. We often overlook that fact because answers are not always what we were looking for or in the time frame we expected, Otherwise. none of us would be here loving one another, supporting one another, and caring for one another. If prayers were not answered, we would not have survived those times of impossible adversity and situations which appeared to be so controlling.

We are not here to judge. That is in God's hands. We are here to say goodbye to our father. In this farewell, the seeming paradox of God's plan becomes clearer. None of us will ever have to wonder about the value of a human life. Seventy-nine years, twelve children, twenty-six grandchildren and twenty-three great grandchildren after his birth, our father leaves us. Regardless of circumstances, situations and all negatives he has left us with far better than we could have imagined when our questions seemed so unanswerable about his legacy. He is a part of us. Without him we would have ever known the feelings, faith and trust we now share.

In closing, I would like to quote a poem I wrote for Jeannie. Never would I have suspected or deemed it appropriate for this occasion, but it now appears to be the most appropriate tribute I can share.

Love is similar to old and worn shoe laces
to rubber bands
and that is more than tender words
and holding hands
Love must be united by a knot that is strong
and though it may slip
from the wear and the pulling
tension and fraying
it does not untie.
Love must be flexible enough
to withstand the pressure
of being stretched between
the wants, needs and misconceptions
of people
and it must be resilient enough
to withstand the trauma
of compromise.
Love may disappear from mind
temporarily
but it is never gone for long
and when it returns
we find it has grown
twice as strong
as when it seemed to leave us
all alone.

Goodbye! DAD

God bless You all.

- *CONSEQUENCES* -

WHEN I WAS A LITTLE CHILD

We are artists.
The canvas on which we paint is imagination
Where perception is never static
Where the strokes and colors of what is intended
Are frequently misinterpreted
And when it comes to description, Webster's is
obsolete.
Translation occurs inside
Where meanings come alive and are felt
in love or hate
in peace or insecurity
And it is here where joy and pain reside.
When I was a little child
I believed sticks and stones could break my bones
But words could never hurt me.
Now,
I am grown and I have found
words not only hurt
but the wounds they bring about
heal much slower than broken bones
if they ever heal - at all.

A STEP AT A TIME

Another day
Yesterday has evolved
And what did not happen
Is either missed
Or new opportunity.
I am in,
that realm
Where we say we all want to be
And am reminded of youthful
Idealistic ignorance
When I believed
Choice was easy
To blunder blindly
Was crusading
Getting things done
misleading
Which ultimately
Led to agony.
Agony of the soul
Over price paid
And inflation yet to be paid.
Regardless of circumstance
Or consequences
Decisions must be made.
The greatest truth is
The worst price to pay
Is made
By making no decision at all.

FERTILE FIELDS

Unto each a season,
What would Capistrano be
Without the swallows

The center line divides a journey by half
And dead ends are only reached
When we refuse to turn around.
Detours ...
Ah, detours
What would shadows in the mind conceal
Without those junctures
Plateaus
Where decisions are made
Superhighways
Through which
Fertile fields of wonder
Are discovered
On the other side 0f
Congested stop signs
Right of ways yielded
And beyond the light of caution
Reflecting memories from color red
When green was the only way to go.

Consequences
Oh, consequences
Life lasting, threatening
Controlling

What might have been
Could have ...
What is.

How? How?   How?

Dreams should not be forsaken
For questions that never end.
Hope is more than the unknown
Hiding behind the illusions
Of life's dead ends

It rains. I dream of Sunny skies.
I cry. I recall, seek, need laughter.
Depression settles in
But I have known the uphill side
Of such conditioning
Pain is a bitter, jealous, selfish
Psychosis
Or a conditioning
Forging, growing
Metamorphosis
Leading to dreams
Substance to life
And direction to
Fields of wonder yet be wandered.

PROMISE

What have I given up getting here?
Some questions are only answered
By where the mind is at.
Regardless
Actions or consequences
My mind is never content
With staying where I am at.

If there is
Another sun to rise
Another poem to write
Another dream to dream
I haven't given up.
The cup is only empty
awaiting
the process of being filled
with what is yet to be
I go forward
No regrets or remorse
Over a cup emptied of
What was given up ...

If what lies ahead
Is worse
That is the set of my sail.
As long as I steer the course
And run aground
That will be no bitter pill
Though I failed.

Know joy
Be happy
In life's travails
It isn't in what is given up
But in how we sailed
That tells
What ultimately prevails.

CULTIVATION - HARVESTING

Illusion is truth untarnished by reality
Promise of love
Hope, prejudice
Discrimination, credit
Genius, emotion
Sex, advertising
Alcohol, drugs, tobacco
Good times, compromise
Greener pastures
Running in the fast lane
Easy money, assumption
Utopia
Absent consequences.

Delusion is assigning value
Giving into or living with
Reality of illusion turned sour.
It is propaganda
Hiding paying the piper
Whose time is opposite
Of the symphony promised
For composition.
Delusion is aftermath of moments
Affecting lifetime
A hell in reality
Conditioning controlling behavior.

Yet, when survived
These same infernos
Can forge and hone bright realities.
Most miracles go unnoticed.
They occur in the boredom of time
In absence of rhyme
And midst despair and tension
Hiding the birth of better times.
Fields of wonder grow
In the harshness of reality
Through cultivation
And harvesting of crops surviving
Despite odds saying
Seeds should have died
Not be alive and thriving.

What is love
Until it has survived
Grown from
Matured or regressed
From the tests?

What is success
Until it has overcome
The bitterness of failure
To make it the best?

What is strength
That has never known
Weakness?

Illusion is a field of dreams
The anticipation of expectation
A birthplace for hopes and wishes.

Delusion is a factory manufacturing
Market place for sharing existence
Opposite the reality suggested, implied
Or promised.

PRESSURES

I am not combating outside
evil influences on my life.
The pressures coming to bear
are from choice, or the results
of not having exercised
any choice at all,
and I think
consequences of the latter
the greatest and most difficult
consequence
of all.

- *TIRED* -

LOST

*It is a terrible state
to be lost geographically
but the worst loss
lost can be
is being lost
midst faceless people
emotionally.*

A FISH OUT OF WATER

As a fish out of water struggles for air
or a fledgling bird leaves the nest to survive
I try to keep alive hopes, dreams - desire.
However, unlike those whose fate is destined
I can exist in an unnatural habitat.
My emotional barometers, perception
and personality have an uncanny resilience
for being stretched between the extremes
without becoming too much one or the other.

I have sought from each disappointment
a patience and perseverance
preparing me for the next,
and from each pain I have learned
there is an offsetting pleasure to be enjoyed.
But there are the times
when being alive seems muddled and addled.
Times like now, when,
the wondering isn't wonder and
the nightmares certainly cannot
be called dreams any more.

The creative side of my mind
appears to be canceled.
Not because I love any less
but because I seem incapable
of loving any more.

It hurts and is hard
to be optimistic when
all there is to give
is never enough.

How far
can human understanding
be stretched?

I don't know. I only know
if I can make it
to tomorrow, chances are
I shall be okay.

QUEST

God!
I am tired
of walking through
valleys
and of shadows
I have seen enough.
I am having
a time not fearing
evil.
The only thing
keeping me going
inspite
of messing up,
is You
are with me
and on me
You have not
given up.
Without Your
blessed Son
I would have
no way
of knowing
the faith
that leads
me on
in hope.

Help me keep
my eyes
on the mountain tops
I have been
looking down too long.
May I praise
Your name from
way up there
as I have
desperately
cried for You
in despair.
I celebrate your being
and for the living
I have done,
I pray
to linger in
the light of Jesus
until all my time
on Earth is done.

Though I grow
weary and the weight
heavier,
I walk, I crawl

I'll go on.
If You have not
given up on me,
I can do nothing else.
Though
I plod
I'll praise
Your name
my almighty
wonderful, caring
loving
God!

DIVIDENDS ... JOY

I know I want peace.
But what is peace?

It certainly is not what
I once would have said
it was.
Then I was so simple
as to visualize
quite absent of worry,
no monetary strain
and love without
restraint or
reservations -
The dictionary
I just referenced
defines peace as,
"a state of rest
or tranquility; calm;
freedom from war
or disturbance;
spiritual content,
but like love as
defined by Webster's
I have grown beyond
categorized definitions
and the peace I'd
like to know

is much broader,
much deeper
and very very personal.

It has to do
with attitude
regardless of rest,
tranquility, calm, war,
disturbance or searching for
spiritual content -
It has to do
with a way of living,
accepting consequence
and being happy
inspite of the severest
circumstance.
It has to do
with understanding
if for no other reason
than the questions
that lead to
misunderstanding are
unimportant to ask.
It has to do with being
because there is
no greater joy
than being.

Peace like love
is an attitude.
It is a state
of mind that
can be found
only inside one's
self. It
can neither be taught
nor bought
and its greatest
quality is the
multiplication and
division of itself
when it is shared.
Peace and love
can never exist
unto themselves.
They are attributes
that exist for
the sole purpose
of paying dividends
among two or more,
and the possession
of their wisdom
demands an extension
which the selfish
would view as
subtraction. But.

The selfish are
always confounded
by the magic of
giving somehow
ending up as
addition.

I want to know happiness
so I may
soothe unhappiness.
I want to know laughter
so I may
somehow help quell fears
and dry tears -
I want to know forgiveness
so I may
have the forbearance
understanding and love
to forgive.
I pray to understand
though I may
be sorely misunderstood.
I hope to be
here and now-
knowing there is
no greater discovery than
life is only important
exciting and unfolding
where my feet are at.

I have been from
here to there.
I have witnessed
the disappointment
of greener grass.
I walk on the
pathway of
moments that hold
no greater potential
for wonder
than the astonishment
and amazement
I behold
if my eyes will see
my brain interpret
and my sense of
expression
will share
as I walk.
Time, pleasure ...
joy ...
Neither need be worried
about nor pursued.
As long as
my senses are
alive,
they surround me.
Peace
I know
I have found you.

LET ME SPLASH AND SPLATTER

There has to be a bottom

Dear God!

My God!

There has to be a bottom

Please!

Bring it up

Surprise me.

I am tired of this
Uncontrolled descent
Bouncing off
One stair tread
to another.

Blame
Is all on me.
But
I'm not going to stop
Looking for more.
I'm not going to stop
Loving or giving
When I can.

I'm going to hit the bottom
And splat or bounce
I'm going squeeze
Every ounce of pleasure
There is
From Living
giving, taking
Sharing
until consequences
Get better
or there is no choice
And worst is all that's left.

I'm going to care for every worry
Appreciate every smile
Share them through listening
Forgiveness and understanding.

Nothing, no
circumstance
Is going to make me
Curse or abandon you.
My
Strengths, weaknesses
Assets, liabilities
Tears, laughter
Joy, depression

Transgressions
Repentance
Regressions, growth
Hate, love
Are yours.

God!

Dear God!

If there is a bottom
Bring it up

Let it hit me

PLEASE

Let me get
On my way to up.

THEATER

Love is mostly defined
in utopian ways,
but it is both
positive and negative -
smiles and tears -
and if this seems
a paradox
it's only because love
is never definable
on an
all-inclusive basis.
Some of the truest
acts of love
go unrecognized
and end up midst
seeming destruction
with no one
but the actor
understanding.
Love is personal.
It can be stunted
as well as mature
and growing.

Sometimes it
has to go beyond
the vision of dreams
before its force
is appreciated.
Existence is not enough.
Even stunted love
is made of stronger stuff.
In retrospect
what, when, where
and how
are easy to see.
Why is the important
thing for us.
to try and grasp
to pass on
in all of love's tragedies.

HOPE FOR TOMORROW

Yesterday may not have been
What was wished
But it brought us here.
We make
wrong right
Bad good
Be
Caring
Loving
Reason for living
Hope for tomorrow
Worthwhile.

I avoid you
Not socially, intellectually
Superficially
Circumstance, consequence
Bind, blind

Memories ago
I could not have loved you
As I do.
Pleasure disappeared
Disappointment
Entered in.
I had neither
Knowledge nor patience
To tell me
Hurt dividing
And pain growing
Is as lasting for two
As for one.
When the want is here
Mutually
Words are not needed
Ties that bind are grown
And we draw breath
To breathe again.

MOONBEAMS

Shadows chase the sun to twilight
Night begins to glow in mellow moonlight
The moonbeams bathe our love
with warmth that comes from within.
The quiet of night -
Its images illusive to sight -
is for dreaming and hoping.
The day's traumas are softened -
laughter is natural -
anticipation for pleasure is heightened.

- LISTEN TO THE WHISPER -

LOVE AND LAUGHTER

Listen to the whisper of hope
If we shall listen
it never disappears,
and at times
of love and laughter
it shouts
at least temporarily
that promises and dreams
of wonder are kept.

MEMORIES OF DREAMS

Listen to the whisper.
Thank God
it reappears
and at times
of hate and sadness
in times
of deepest depression
there are
memories
of dreams
and wonder
once met.

TIME AND CIRCUMSTANCE

Listen to the whisper.
When it is hard to cope
During
deepest depression
it speaks of time
and circumstance
through memories
of dreams
and wonder once met.

THEY WHISPER SOFTLY

Listen to the memories.
They had to be made.
They whisper softly
and tell from having been
as long
as there is hope
there is a promise
that a sense
of wonder
in dreams
can still be felt.

- *EPILOGUE* -

MY LINK TO THE CHAIN OF LOVE

Height, width. depth and breadth of eternity may never be full, but a contribution to its void is made because of every soul conceived. We are blessed or cursed by our participation. Good or bad, there is no erasure.

I wander through genealogical outlines.
The meanings of my ancestry
begins to develop characters
Beyond the mysteries
of shadows hidden in the mystic of history.
It is as if I discover
paths allowing me to review the darkness of the past,
Yet forward
as I journey into the unknown promise
of the future
and how it will unfold.
It foreshadows
the promises and disappointments
all generations faced
face and will face.
It foretells
value,
glory or futility
of a single life
is told
in how
IT IS LIVED.

Seems trite that it has taken 81 years to write this.
maybe I have been blinded
by the ravages of living.
I have been trying
to find answers to the same old questions
Asked as far back as my ancestors lived.
I have looked into thousands of years and
unknown generations
To arrive at the conclusion
God made us in HIS image
So, we can generationally begin
over and over to deliver simple truth ...
WE need to live and pass our story
To love one another as we would have others love us.
And to know collectively we each
hold the key to growth and acceptance
Or the power for regression and destruction.

Let us each seek our own salvation
And journey toward our quests for Heaven or Hell
But until we see from way up there
Or from way down there
The simple value of loving one another
The journey becomes more complicated
For our descendants.
History multiplies the unanswered questions
By expansion of progress
Multiplication of societies

Growth in intellect
diversity and challenges from
technology, society
medicine and choices
guarantying such
complications.

Be what you want to be.
Do what you want to do.
Have, give, share and care
Conflicts with
Get, keep and hoard
As it always has.
But is so much more complicated
than when we began
With the first hatching of the egg of mankind (humans)
and as generations have added up.
We are all but dashes between birth and death on a
tombstone,
But unlike any of God's other creatures
we can influence the mystery symbolized.

As I struggle to be a good person. Husband, Father,
friend whose story my descendants will review positively
because God blesses me with the gift to reveal …

A few more days of life
I Pray
All of us
Live all our days knowing
we are EACH worthwhile.

ABOUT THE AUTHOR

Beecher B Brown Jr

I am 81. Life in all its, pleasures, paradoxes, challenges, adversities and promises has been good to me. Strangely this has developed into a time for looking ahead rather than back. Ahead to what the future holds for our children and their participation in developing through the mysteries and mistakes of life. I began thinking I knew a lot and been taught lessons learned was a mutual process, I learned to be a better listener, to be more understanding and to know the redemption of forgiveness and to accept both my own and their successes and failures in the passage of time.

Jeannie and I are better grandparents than we were parents. The passage of time, blessings of forgiveness and hope for the future is held in the hands of future generations as it was passed to us to from our parent's link to God's chain of love. It is my prayer, what I write is more than a recollection of random thoughts, but will tell a story of who I was, who I am and who I would like you to know as I enter the final attempts to forge fiber and strength to the link Jeannie and I will bequeath by living in and through God's mysteries.

I went to the University of Tennessee, served three years in the US Army, have been in the Insurance business, sold banking and commer¬cial products and designed, manufactured and marketed displays for various industries out of flat sheet plastics. I retired from Target in 2017. It is a blessing to participate in mankind's history.

Love of God, family and friends are my motivations and inspira¬tions. All I find worthy of sharing is influenced by them. I hope something I share has meaning and brings joy to someone in need of it.

www.amazon.com/author/beecherbrown

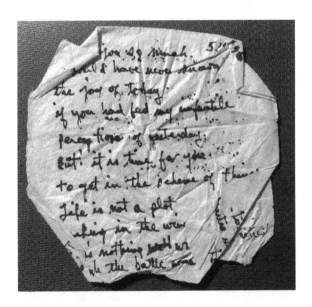

The Beecher B Brown
Older Than Dirt
eBook Collection

Available on Amazon.com

Also on Amazon.com
in both eBook and Paperback

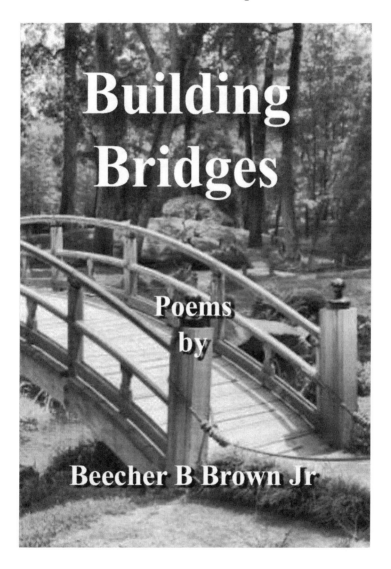

Also on Amazon.com
in both eBook and Paperback

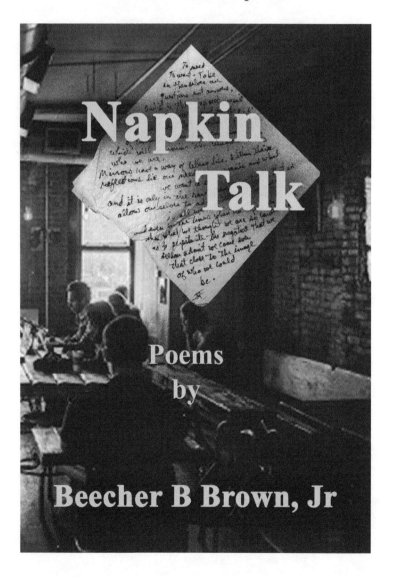

Made in the USA
Columbia, SC
10 November 2023

25771642R00083